Secrets of the Nether Moor

Allison Tebo

Secrets of the Nether Moor
By Allison Tebo

All rights reserved. No part of this book may be reproduced or transmitted in any form or by any means, electronic or mechanical, including photocopying or recording or by any information storage and retrieval systems, without expressed written consent of the author and/or artists.

Secrets of the Nether Moor is a work of fiction. Names, characters, places, and incidents are products of the author's imagination. Any resemblance to actual events or persons, living or dead, is entirely coincidental.

Story copyright owned by Allison Tebo
Cover illustration by James @ GoOnWrite.com
Cover design by Marcia A. Borell

First Printing, March 2025

Hiraeth Publishing
P.O. Box 1248
Tularosa, NM 88352
e-mail: hiraethsubs@yahoo.com

Visit www.hiraethsffh.com for online science fiction, fantasy, horror, scifaiku, and more. Stop by our online bookstore for novels, magazines, anthologies, and collections. **Support the small, independent press...and your First Amendment rights.**

For Anne: a spooky connoisseur, a fellow adventurer, and the dearest of friends. Let's visit Romney Marsh for real someday!

Secrets of the Nether Moor

The night was full of clouds, their edges silver-plated from where the moon shone behind their scudding mass. But the slivers of moonlight did little to illuminate the moor, leaving it a dark sea of waving grass and hidden things half-lost in shadow.

The night coach from North Hampstead rattled down the narrow dirt road that cut through the Nether Moor's otherwise impassable breadth—a pale thread winding its way through the windy gloom. Inside the coach, pressed close to the window, Charlotte Morrison looked out into the night and then down at the handbag cradled in her lap. She placed her arms over it, enfolding it as carefully as if it were an unhatched egg, and praying that it would not go off before she was out of the carriage.

There, resting in her handbag, was a bomb. Not an ordinary bomb, thank goodness, but an explosive component nonetheless. A spell bomb.

A tiny orb of what looked like copper, but wasn't copper, full of some thick dusty component that looked like grain, but wasn't grain. There would be an explosion that wasn't really an explosion—and then havoc.

The mechanized-carriage clattered on down the road. The robotic driver's low hum of gears could only be dimly heard over the creak of the wheels, intermingling with the grumbling of the brutish guard, who sat beside the automaton armed with a blunderbuss and a stream of complaints that would have repelled anyone or anything. Except the automaton, who cheerily counted down the miles for his passengers, oblivious to the hired gunman beside him and the roughness of the road.

With every bump and clatter, Charlotte sighed and cringed, imagining the spell going off without warning, even though the old woman had assured her it wouldn't go off without Charlotte first pulling the string.

The carriage thudded over a stone and Charlotte flinched and looked into the night, wondering if there was anyone she knew out there.

She was friends with some of the harmless old recluses that lived on the edges of the moor, the ones who made a living selling homemade potions. It was whispered that these individuals were hiders of elves, communers with monsters, and friends of Jack O'Lantern. Those friendships were the nearest Charlotte had ever come to rebelling against anything. While visiting one, she had dropped a hint that she was interested in spell bombs. What had followed had been a hair-raising meeting in the middle of the night with the friend of a friend— a wizened old woman who looked as if she might have been a troll, but was doing her best to hide it beneath a hat.

The terrified but determined Charlotte had received her desired object for a modest fee: a round, coppery sphere tucked in a gauzy bag with a bit of fuse sticking out of the top.

Charlotte had held it as if it had been . . . well . . . a bomb. "It won't hurt anyone, will it?"

The old woman, sucking industriously at a potion pill of unrevealed properties, waved a hand in dismissal. "The spell itself won't hurt anyone. What people do when they're enchanted, that's another matter. One never knows what to expect. Every mortal reacts differently. I've known some to start raving, others to attack their neighbors, and a few to fall in love with complete strangers. You shall definitely cause confusion. But watch yourself, young lady. It might have been easier just to cosh these chaps. But then, that's none of my business. Thank you again for your patronage. You make illegal bartering possible."

Remembering those ominous words now, Charlotte looked around anxiously at her carriage mates. She certainly didn't fancy seeing any of them raving, let alone trying to shoot or kiss her. Just a few moments of confusion was all she needed, and then she would dare to slip the letter from Pegg's bag, and make her escape.

She had at least had the foresight to get a temporary disguise potion from the woman, who very nicely offered her a two-for-one discount."

Charlotte had been singularly squeamish at the thought of taking the potion—she was rather attached to her face. But, in the end, fear of arrest outweighed her fear of magic.

She had taken it in private, which was the one smart thing she had done that night, since the uncomfortable transformation had caused her to be sick, and then to scream when she looked into a mirror and saw another face looking back at her.

Charlotte reached up weak fingers and traced her mouth. After all of this, she had *better* succeed. She clung miserably to the hope that the potion would indeed wear off sometime, preferably before her aunt saw her at breakfast tomorrow.

The wheels turned and Charlotte's thoughts tumbled end over end as she looked out the cracked window. The moors rolled away beneath the star-specked sky, miles upon miles of marsh and reeds.

And monsters.

Home to reed crawlers, will o' the wisps, and water crones. No one ventured across the marsh at night, except for Jack O Lantern.

If he had been out tonight, Charlotte would have appreciated it if he would ride her way.

But he couldn't help her or save her. Not when he was behind bars.

Thinking of it again made Charlotte's heart sink. Like most East Enders, Charlotte had been hearing stories of the great Jack O' Lantern for years. As the middle class was taxed beyond all endurance and press gangs swept the countryside to steal the young men of the dale to force them into the Party's navy, someone had decided to make a strike for freedom.

This daring adventurer and outlaw rode the moors—even at night. Being the last of the elven race, he was either welcome amongst the creatures, or at the very least, held great powers of persuasion over them. He was known only by the name Jack O' Lantern, for his lamp could be seen some nights, traversing the moors that no human dared to travel.

His name was carved on trees, spelled out with pebbles. His fair and clean-shaven elven features, with his pointed ears and long hair, decorated many chalkboards and many dirt paths. He was the darling of every man, woman, and child—be they human or brownie or minotaur or dwarf.

In the eyes of the law, Jack O' Lantern was a criminal and a rogue, but to the people, he was a hero. Countless citizens owed their livelihoods, their homes, and even their survival to Jack. His daring deeds had inspired many a person in these parts to fight back against tyranny.

But the day that no one had really believed could happen had finally come to pass. Jack O' Lantern, the hero of the people, had been arrested.

And so the people grew quiet, waiting and hoping. With their champion in shackles, the countryside watched uneasily to see what would happen next, and tried to keep up their hope that the resistance against a tyrannical government would live on, despite the capture of their unofficial leader.

Charlotte wrung her hands. With Jack captured, his men must surely be working on a way to free him. Which was good, but it meant that the ordinary people that Jack and his crew usually looked after were neglected. Someone had to help those people while he was gone.

Somehow, tonight, that someone had become Charlotte Morrison.

I can't do this, I'm not a hero. That's Richard's role—not mine.

When they had been children, it had always been her brother who pretended to be Jack O' Lantern, while Charlotte had uncomplainingly played the role of helpless victim. She had never, ever, wanted to play Jack O' Lantern.

But Richard had patterned his life off the legend. Charlotte had once watched, petrified, as her brother stopped on the way home from church to give a bully the greatest drubbing of his life.

As her brother walked back, out of breath but head high, he saw Charlotte's look and said, kindly. "Sometimes you have to hurt bad men to save good ones."

Those words ran through Charlotte's head now. She could only hope that she would not be forced to hurt anyone tonight.

She steadied her handbag with one hand, and she was sure she didn't imagine the fact that her fingers tingled. She resisted the urge to check her pocket watch or look out the window and looked around the carriage instead.

The four corners of the interior of the carriage were lit by miniature lanterns. Their orange glow illuminated the faces of the six people who—hopefully—had no idea of what she was about to do to them. Even more, Charlotte was hoping that they wouldn't remember it when she did.

According to the moor people, victims would have a very vague—and thoroughly uncomfortable—memory of how they had behaved, but it was unlikely that they would remember what anyone else had done. Or, if they did, they would never be so presumptuous as to mention it. Charlotte was trusting in that.

Charlotte's wavering gaze darted to *him*— Major Ebenezer Pegg. Every time her eye caught on those hard features, she flinched. It was a face that looked as if it had been carved from a block of stone. The small grey eyes were as easy to read as an ugly government notice. Pegg not only didn't care that he held an innocent life in his hands, he would relish snuffing it out.

It had taken all of Charlotte's resolve to step into the carriage when she had seen him sitting there in the shadows. It was only when she thought of Richard that she had the strength to take her seat, and commit herself to whatever lay ahead.

Beside Pegg was his aide, Lieutenant Brackenberry. He was handsome in a kind of wooden way—rather like an old statute, one that was crumbling about the edges from the powerful force beside him.

Miss Nicholson sat beside him. She was a thin woman with glasses and a severe expression that matched the severity of her clothes and hair. She had revealed to Charlotte that she was a private tutor—and made it clear by her attitude that she disapproved of young ladies who traveled at night without chaperones.

Miss Nicholson was chaperoned by Sophie Beekel, a two-foot brownie with a squashy face and large nose and mouth that enhanced her own snoring. Brownies were common in these parts, along with minotaur's and dwarves. They were different, but they bore no magical abilities. They were simply odd.

Sophie was the only passenger that had nodded off—somewhat belying her role as chaperone. Like most brownies, she preferred to sleep upside down and was now catching a few winks by dangling from the rings in the ceiling that were provided for a brownie's convenience, swaying gently back and forth like a piece of meat.

A clergyman with a kindly face sat across from Charlotte. He was the only one who tried to keep up a friendly conversation in the carriage, until the others frigid silence and Charlotte's shyness eventually sent him retreating into silence.

The last passenger was a man in his mid-thirties. He had a solid sort of face, a square unshaven jaw and a queue of ginger colored hair. Charlotte thought he looked nervous. He had got on at the last moment at the previous way station, and Charlotte had almost thought he was going to get right back off again when he saw Pegg and Brackenberry, but he had crunched himself into the far corner at the last moment and put his head down. When the slovenly guard had demanded his name for the roster that every State-controlled carriage was required to fill out before a journey, the stranger had only given the name Bates. The guard had cocked an eyebrow, but he had let the paperwork slide, a fact that Pegg had noticed with a disapproving frown.

Bates hadn't moved or spoken since the journey had begun, except for his eyes. Charlotte could see them gleaming in the dark, darting back and forth.

Charlotte had been hoping it would just be her, Pegg, and his aide on this carriage. She had been unable to do anything but watch in dismay at the way station as the other passengers kept boarding the coach, further complicating her mission with their presence.

The lantern twitched and bobbed in the corners of the carriage and its movement once again had Charlotte thinking of Jack O' Lantern.

She allowed herself a few moments of the wistful daydream that Jack O' Lantern had been freed earlier that day and was even now riding to her aid. Then she plucked up the wish, deposited it in a dark place with shaky determination, and turned her mind sternly to the task ahead.

She couldn't always live expecting someone else to save people in trouble. The day she had most feared—the day her family and Jack O' Lantern were not there to do the rescuing for her—had finally come. And now she had no choice but to screw up her courage and do her best and be her own kind of hero.

And that was where Charlotte had her one small advantage. Richard had a way with words, but Charlotte had a way with the moor and the people who lived on it. And they had a way of knowing what went on in the world.

Old Bess, Charlotte's old friend, who might or might not have been a field gnome, had alerted Charlotte to the rumor. A man named Major Pegg had gotten evidence linking Richard to the Voice of Freedom. How he had gotten it was unknown, but it *was* known that he would taking these papers to Londonium, to sign out a warrant for Richard's arrest, so that he could be waiting for him in the youth's hometown when Richard returned from his current business venture.

Old Bess had been instrumental in letting Charlotte know what carriage route Pegg would be taking and in putting Charlotte in contact with the old crone in the depths of the moor.

Charlotte could only hope that all of their risks would not go to waste.

Out in the night, a queer high-pitched sound pierced the night like a rising wind, growing sharper and sharper until something swept past the open window with a rush of wings—a soft sound followed immediately by the blast of the guard's blunderbuss.

She screamed. She couldn't help it.

The carriage halted with a jerk that caused a flurry of gasps and curses to erupt from the passengers. Sophie swung so wildly from her hooks that her head impacted with Brackenberry, an occurrence that seemed to greatly disturb the Lieutenant but did not a whit to disturb Sophie. Charlotte went flying into the arms of the startled vicar, who grabbed her and kept her from falling to the floor.

The carriage door flew open. The grizzled guard stuck his head in, letting the light of his lantern fall on the disgruntled passengers.

"What's amiss?" he growled. "Who yelled?"

"What was that sound?" the vicar inquired.

"You mean aside from the scream?" the guard groused. "Just a moonbat strike. Drove it off. No problem."

Major Pegg leaned forward to glower at him. "Are you crazy, man? I would have thought a guard would know better than to pause in the middle of the moor. Don't stop, you idiot, drive!"

With a glare for Pegg, the guard slammed the door shut and the carriage jolted as he leaped onto his seat again. A second later, they were off again.

Her carriage mates stared at Charlotte with censure.

"My goodness, child," Miss Nicholson had regained her voice after gasping soundlessly for several seconds and she peered through her spectacles at Charlotte. "Here, take some of this *sal volatile*." She whisked a bottle from her valise. "It will calm your nerves."

Charlotte eyed the bottle cap that Miss Nicholson held out to her and reflected grimly that it would take a barrel of *sal volatile* to calm her nerves, but she took the proffered cap and downed the mixture meekly. If she had planned on keeping a low profile, she was doing a dreadful job of it. No one forgot a traveling companion who screamed at random moments.

The vicar leaned forward with a kindly air. "Is this your first time across the moor, my dear?"

Charlotte nodded. She didn't travel much outside her own hamlet. Although it wasn't the moor that was frightening her tonight—but she couldn't tell any of them that.

The vicar patted her hand. "I've crossed twenty times, and come out safe and sound."

Charlotte offered him a grateful glance, and resisted the urge to ask him if he had ever attacked a government officer with a spell bomb to rob him of incriminating papers and, if so, how had he managed to keep his skin intact? But she kept her mouth shut.

"What takes you to East End?" he inquired.

"My brother needs me," she whispered faintly, holding the words close to her beating heart.

The vicar smiled at her. "Well, you're a brave girl to go to him across the moor. He's lucky to have you for a sister."

"Thank you."

"We'd be even luckier if certain people would keep quiet," Pegg grumbled rudely.

Brackenberry, once more looking politely apologetic for his barbarous commanding officer, leaned forward and murmured. "Don't worry, miss—we'll protect you."

Charlotte offered him a wan smile and resisted the urge to ask who would protect *him*.

She gripped her handbag and closed her eyes and wished like a small child hanging hopes on stars that Jack O' Lantern would appear. Someone, anyone, better suited to this than her.

Jack O' Lantern had always been a role model for her brother, someone for him to aspire to. To Charlotte, Jack had been a kind of fairy—the magic solution to all of her difficulties, not someone to pattern herself after.

But now she would have to. To save her brother, she would have to start thinking and acting like Jack O' Lantern.

Just do it. Richard is counting on you.

Charlotte's heart raced. The other day, when Charlotte had discovered the truth of who her brother really was, she had asked

Richard why he did it, what drove him to take such risks.

"The true fighters need encouragement. They can lose heart if they think they're alone."

Charlotte had only found out by accident and promised to keep his secret. Surely it wasn't so dangerous, and surely Richard would soon give it up.

But it was dangerous, and he hadn't given it up. And now she was following in his footsteps.

She was risking her life, but that didn't mean she was crazy. She, out of everyone in town, might have dared to traverse the moor in the day—but at night? Only a fool would do such a thing. Or Jack O' Lantern himself. Every East Ender knew the way to survive out here: stay on the road. And that was why she must wait, in a fever of agony, until they reached the Crossroads—until she had some hope of escaping, as well as surviving.

About three miles across the moor, there was the Nether Crossroads—the one place in all the moor where the four roads, built by monumental effort across enchanted grounds, intersected.

It was at the Crossroads that Charlotte would take her chance. She would find some excuse to stop the carriage, get outside, throw the bomb through the window, steal the papers, and then slip away down the road. Simple. It would be a long walk through the dark, but if she stayed on a road, she could chance it. She couldn't risk stopping the carriage in the *middle* of the moor. The carriage itself, and everyone in it could be at risk too. One had to keep moving out here. Small rests could be risked at the Crossroads, and small missions carried out. Yes, no matter what happened tonight, it had to happen at the Crossroads.

With that resolution in mind, she decided that she might as well plant the idea of stopping in her companion's heads as soon as possible.

Charlotte rapped on the roof of the carriage to get the driver's attention.

The flap opened, revealing the blank face of the steam-powered automaton driving the coach and, beside him, the brutish guard.

"How long is it to the crossroads?" Charlotte warbled.

"Six miles, madam, which will be thirty minutes," the robot intoned.

"I need you to stop when we get there, please. I feel a little ill," Charlotte announced, blushing a little as she said it.

The automaton lifted its tin top-hat with impersonal affability and then slammed the flap shut.

Charlotte's seat mates gave her wary looks and scooted as far away as they could in the restrictive confines of the carriage.

Lieutenant Brackenberry offered her a peppermint to settle her stomach, Miss Nicholson lent her a fan, and Sophie—waking up for a few groggy moments—moved into the overhead compartment to give Charlotte a clear shot through the window.

Charlotte blushed harder and murmured her thanks while simultaneously trying not to feel guilty about what she would really do to these people. They weren't bad folk; it was a pity she had to spell them.

Except for Pegg.

Pegg speared her with a cold look. "I'm in a hurry, young woman. You had better not delay us!"

"I won't, sir," Charlotte whispered, shrinking into her seat. But in her heart, a little flame of dislike flared to life, fueling on her determination to see this mission through.

A shocked gasp from Nicholson caused everyone in the carriage to look at her.

She had been rooting around in her valise for some undisclosed property and she was now dead-white as she removed her hand from her bag. She held out a pamphlet as if it might bite her and darted one panicked look at Pegg. "I—I didn't put that in my valise. I don't know where it came from."

Pegg sucked in his breath as if she had thrown poison into the air. "One of those Voice of Freedom bits of rubbish?" Pegg snatched the pamphlet from Nicholson and crumpled it in his fist. "It is illegal to possess such pamphlets, miss. You had better have a good explanation for why you're carrying that."

The vicar stirred. "Just a moment there, Major," he said, his benign voice rather sharp. But when the Major glared at him, he was all sweetness again as he felt about in his pocket. "It's not just Miss Nicholson who appears to have one. Bless my soul, it seems *I* have one too." Only the vicar didn't look dismayed as he handed the forbidden object to Pegg. His look was almost affectionate.

Curious, Charlotte felt automatically in her pocket and squeaked when her hand touched paper.

"I—so do I." Her mind spun. Had Richard put it there this morning?

Pegg pulled it from her hand and Charlotte let go reluctantly, somehow feeling that she was letting go of Richard.

"Is that all of them?" Pegg demanded. His eye fell on Bates. The nervous man flushed and then searched his pockets hastily.

"I have one as well," he muttered, handing it over to Pegg.

Pegg grabbed it from him with a suspicious look. "These are illicit materials." He tore the pile into pieces and threw it out the window. Charlotte watched the bits of paper flutter away into the dark.

Pegg glared at Sophie, as if willing her to wake up and turn over any non-government approved papers, but she slumbered on, oblivious. He addressed the others instead.

"I would advise you all to watch yourself. Even the possession of such materials is not viewed kindly by the Council."

The vicar leaned forward. "Out of curiosity, do you or the lieutenant happen to have a pamphlet on your person?"

"How dare you suggest such an impenitent—" Pegg began, and then his voice faltered as the embarrassed Brackenberry turned out his own pocket and found a pamphlet.

"Curses," Pegg snarled, snatching it from the Brackenberry and subsiding briefly into silence. Everyone noticed that he did not turn out his own pockets, just as they noticed the angry flush when he brushed a hand over a slight bulge in his coat.

He swore again, more vehemently this time, and Miss Nicholson glared at him. He didn't notice her disapproval.

"Rank impudence," he muttered. "Some may view it as amusing to scatter illegal and dangerous reading material about, but I assure you it's no joke. It is a crime against the State."

The others listened silently. All government officials assumed that any civilian anywhere near a supposed crime was not only culpable but somehow responsible. Even in her sheltered life, Charlotte had been exposed to this tirade before—but never had she hated it so deeply. Before that accidental discovery yesterday morning in her brother's study, she hadn't known Richard was the author of the Voice of Freedom. Tonight, the bureaucratic rebuke against the pamphlets author was personal, and she hated it with every fiber of her being.

Pegg folded his arms. "A very clever joke, but whoever is responsible for this won't be laughing tomorrow. This will be the last night these cursed pamphlets are ever circulated, and the last night the so-called Voice of Freedom remains at large. I'll put a stick in his wheel." Pegg clapped a hand to the satchel at his waist.

Charlotte was sure her face would give her away then as all her anger and horror rushed to her face in a wave of burning heat.

But it wasn't her expression that had caught the Major's attention.

"You disapprove, vicar?" Pegg asked sharply.

The vicar did not move or blink. "Perhaps. It's my job to extend mercy. When you've lived as long as I have, you see that people do the things they do for a variety of reasons."

Pegg glared at him. "Extend mercy, if you will, on the parishioners that rob the poor box, but leave these rebels to me. These are no mere criminals, but a dangerous canker. They balk against paying due taxes, they shirk from their duty to the State by hiding their young men from the press gangs. And they hide that blaggard who calls himself the Voice of Freedom. Freedom—bah. Anarchy is what he preaches. He is stirring up civil war with all his empty-headed rhetoric about our government being too powerful and it being against the law to infringe on the people's personal rights. He's a madman, and a disease."

Charlotte stared at him as he so easily pronounced judgment on a youth he did not know, but one she had known all her life. None of those accusations were true, and yet, in the eyes of the government, the most selfless and kind person Charlotte knew was a criminal. Her throat swelled from the pressure of holding back an angry sob.

". . . It is because the government is so powerful that we keep the supposedly oppressed people safe from the oppression of illegal magic wielders. Isn't that right Brackenberry, ay? Ay?"

Brackenberry jumped, clearly not listening very closely, and said dutifully. "Indeed, sir."

"That's right." Pegg was silent a moment, like a dog gnawing at a bone before he burst into words again. "The people indeed. Tch! If they listen to rabble like this they have no business to ask for personal rights, no business thinking, no business existing. The sooner such rubbish can be drummed out of their skulls the better for the country. Am I right, Brackenberry? Ay? Ay?"

"Yes sir," Brackenberry murmured obediently once more.

The rest of them shrank into silence under this onslaught. Charlotte thought that it was no wonder Richard had found men like this so horrid. It wasn't enough for them to terrorize the people at a distance with far-flung edicts. People like Pegg took it upon themselves to police every individual they encountered, cowing them into agreeing with every government-approved word spoken.

"What's the matter with you?" This was directed sharply at Bates, as Pegg suddenly pivoted his attention and tossed the icy comment out like the thrust of a knife.

Bates, who had been fidgeting and sweating visibly, froze. "Nothing, sir," He muttered.

Pegg studied him with narrowed eyes, a strange smirk flitting across his face as he settled himself more comfortably in his corner, his gaze lingering on Bates for a moment.

If possible, Bates seemed to be sweating even more profusely. Everyone was looking at him now.

Oh dear, thought Charlotte. *I hope he isn't in trouble. If he is, he'll give himself away.*

The coach suddenly lurched as one of the wheels rolled into a deep groove.

They all collectively held their breath, but the coach rolled on, and they all relaxed. They would not be stranded out on the moor. Leastways, not yet.

Just when they were all relaxing, the carriage hit another rut.

Bates shot out a hand to steady Charlotte. As his arm passed in front of Charlotte, steadying her, his sleeve was pushed back and Charlotte found herself looking down at a dark mark that lay briefly exposed in the lantern light.

A small tattoo had been etched onto his wrist. Charlotte recognized it with a swift jerk of her heart. It was an X—the mark used by the government to indicate that they had cancelled out a citizen's existence, and marked them not only as an undesirable, but a criminal against the State.

Charlotte's eyes shot up from the man's wrist to his face, and Charlotte saw the agony and fear in his eyes.

Bates pushed his coat down over his wrist with a swift gesture, his breath whistling between his teeth as he glanced at Major Pegg.

Pegg was looking back at him with a glittering gaze, and Bates' panicked face betrayed him as clearly as if he had spoken aloud.

"An interesting mark you have there on your arm, stranger."

Pegg rapped on the roof of the carriage. The sound cracked through the strained silence of the carriage like a gunshot.

"Driver!" Pegg barked. "Stop the carriage! Brackenberry, bind that man."

His words cut off in a cry as the robot brought the carriage to a halt so abruptly they were all flung against the far wall and into one another's laps.

The roof hatch flew open and the guard stuck his angry head in, roaring like a bear that had just been roused from his sleep.

"What's amiss now?" he demanded.

But before Pegg could answer, Bates leaped for the carriage door.

Pegg bawled up at him. "Brackenberry, seize him!"

Brackenberry leaned forward to grab Bates by the arm, and Bates turned around long enough to drive his boot into the stomach of the unfortunate Brackenberry, sending him hurtling back into the lap of the horrified Miss Nicholson.

The sudden rocking of the carriage had sent Sophie hurtling through the air like a projectile and Pegg found himself with an armful of brownie instead of escaped prisoner.

Sophie, finally roused by her sleep, opened one eye and her sizable mouth and let out a roar that could have put marsh creatures to shame. "Hey now, what's going on?"

In the midst of the confusion, the carriage door was suddenly flung open, but not by Bates. Charlotte couldn't be certain, but she thought she saw the vicar pressing back into his seat swiftly, as if he had leaned forward to reach for the latch.

Bates freed himself at last from Brackenberry's desperate clutches and tumbled out the open door and into the night.

The robot driver's voice boomed from above them. "Sir, I really must insist that you remain in the carriage for your own safety."

"Shoot him!" Pegg shouted. "Shoot that traitor!"

Charlotte pressed against the back of her seat, petrified. *Use the spell bomb.* The thought whisked through her head in a flash.

But if she used the spell bomb now, her chances of escaping were almost negligible. And yet she couldn't just sit there and do nothing. Bates had revealed himself because of *her*. She had to act fast.

If worse came to worst, she would try to lead Bates across the moor and then they would be eaten together and the message would be destroyed with her. She could at least die knowing that she had saved her brother and tried to save another.

She sprang to her feet, nearly knocking her head against the roof of the carriage, and blocked the open door.

Pegg cursed at her, roundly and loudly but Charlotte stood there a moment longer, shaking but resolute.

"Get out of the way!" Pegg roared. Beneath the sudden clamor, Charlotte heard the click of a pistol being cocked.

She threw her cloak wide, obscuring Pegg's view a second longer, whimpering unintelligibly and only just remembered to shout, "I'm going to be sick," before she toppled out the door.

She snatched the bomb from her bag. Cold jolts of power raced through Charlotte's hands and arms and she sucked in her breath and pulled on the cord. The fuse began to whisper. Charlotte tossed the bomb over her shoulder through the open door and slammed it shut before hitting the ground and burying her head in her arms.

Even then, she could see and feel the brilliant flash, full of not just yellow light, but blue, orange, purple, and pink—flames and sparks and spirals of screaming color as the bomb erupted with a whining shriek and the smell of ashes and burnt petals.

The robot driver let out a shrill screech of gears.

"Attention! My sensors have been greatly overloaded, and my optic relays have ceased to function. Please remain seated and calm until I can run a full diagnostic. I repeat, I have lost visual. Please remain seated safely inside the carriage."

Charlotte raised her head, but did not look back towards the pandemonium behind her. Instead, her eyes found the boxy shadow of Bates, stumbling through moor grass.

"Bates, come back!" Charlotte shouted. "It's all right, I've—I've spelled them. Don't go onto the moor, you'll be killed!"

Bates' solid figure chugged on through the darkness, not heeding her cries.

Charlotte staggered to her feet . . . and left the road to follow.

It astounded her that she was far less afraid of running out into the night on the moor than sitting across from Pegg. Running across the moor in the night, she wasn't afraid at all. In that moment, all she could feel was anger. This was the kind of terror men like Pegg instilled. It made people like Bates decide to chance being eaten by marsh creatures rather than be taken alive.

Charlotte did not regret throwing that spell bomb one bit.

"Come back!" Charlotte shouted. "It's all right!" *Was* it safe for Bates back at the carriage? Only if the spell had really worked. If it hadn't, she might be luring him back to be captured. But if she let him go, he would die.

She stumbled and sloshed her way after him, then stiffened as a muffled cry floated back to her. She dimly saw the shadowy form of Bates go down, as if he had fallen, and the darker shadow of his body was replaced with the flare of a yellow-green glow.

Charlotte bit her lip. Bates had stumbled into a nest of glow flies.

She picked her way carefully over the little islands of turf that floated in the muck and mire of the moor. As she drew closer, she saw that Bates was lying face down in the mud, surrounded by a swarm of the dreaded glow flies.

She fought back her first instinct to yell and run at them while waving her arms. That would only cause them to turn and attack her too.

She knew that if she didn't act fast, the glow flies would sting Bates mercilessly, injecting more and more venom into his veins until he fell into such a deep coma his heart would cease to beat.

A few of the flies broke away from the swarm surrounding Bates and dove towards Charlotte, and the rest of the swarm quickly followed to confront their new threat.

Charlotte stood still. Sudden movements irritated glow flies. She could understand that. A stranger stomping on top of your nest in the middle of the night was upsetting to anybody.

She hummed, low in her throat, that single undulating note that Old Bess had taught her when she was just a little girl, the sound that could sooth the glow flies into a dreamy stupor.

She hummed louder, and the swarm's buzzing died to a murmur as they floated around her curiously.

Charlotte held out a hand, letting the glow flies nudge it. One settled on her knuckles for a moment, crawling across her thumb, its legs brushing her skin. But it did not sting her.

You've got a fine way with the moor, miss. Sometimes I think you are part elf yourself, Old Bess had told Charlotte many a time with a pleased smile.

*I hope she was righ*t, Charlotte thought. The hairs on the back of her neck prickled, but the sensation was more one of wonder than fear as the glow flies surged around her, surrounding her in their shrill sibilance and brilliance. It sounded a like a hundred tiny snores. The humming had worked.

Still humming, and moving cautiously, Charlotte grabbed Bates by the arm and rolled him onto his back to keep him from drowning, doing her best to flop him over carefully to avoid stirring up the flies again. They hissed as Bates' hand slapped into the mud and Charlotte hummed louder until they calmed down once more.

She began dragging him backwards, moving gently. Her cloak kept getting in her way, her shoes sank into the muck, and Bates was astoundingly heavy.

As she pulled, she looked around into the night for anything else that might be watching, though there was no way to tell what might be out here until it was on top of you. Wind slithered across her cheeks and she fought back the cough as she continued to weave the calming note of sound.

Slowly, the cloud of glow flies sank down into the grass, gilding the edges of the scrub and briars until it looked as if a small fuzzy star rested at Charlotte's feet. Then the cloud was left behind, a smudge of light in the muddy darkness as Charlotte finally dragged Bates onto the road. She slumped over his body, exhausted. Now that she was back on the relative safety of the road, new predicaments rapidly reasserted themselves in her tired mind.

Once she got Bates into the carriage, then what? As soon as the spell wore off, Pegg would arrest the man. She had to convince the robot to drive on and then stop at the crossroads, perhaps, and smuggle Bates away there. But how? She didn't have a horse, and she couldn't possibly drag him all the way back home.

Tears of frustration pricked her eyes as she stood over Bates' body, irresolute and caked in mud. The moor pressed close, waiting for her to make a decision, and odd noises reaching her from within the carriage.

"Please return to the carriage immediately," the driver intoned. His visual sensors must have finally cleared, for when Charlotte glanced over her shoulder, his little pinprick eyes were staring at her with mechanical censure. "It is not safe to leave the road."

"I *know* that," Charlotte muttered. She looked down at Bates and noticed that one last stray fly clung to her skirts, like a bit of stardust. Charlotte shook her gown gently and sent it spinning off into the shadows, still humming under her breath to ensure that it did not stir from its dreamy state.

She had made it. She had actually left the road and survived. And she had even retrieved Bates.

Maybe everything would be all right after all?

She looked around. The world was quiet, save for the shushing of the wind through the grass. The coachman sat immovable and placid atop the carriage, waiting for her to follow his instruction. Charlotte noticed that the guard was missing and she looked in all directions, half-expecting to see the scruffy guard running at her from the shadows to echo the robot's scolding, but he was nowhere to be seen.

The moon shone down on the still carriage, and caused shadows to drift over the now-silent windows.

Charlotte looked at the vehicle apprehensively and, shielding her nose and mouth with her elbow in case there was any remaining spell dust floating in the air, she gathered her courage and pulled the carriage door open. She peered in.

The vicar, poor man, was on the floor. To Charlotte's intense discomfiture, Brackenberry and Nicholson had their arms around each other.

"Your hair shines so beautifully in the moonlight, my dear," Brackenberry was murmuring tenderly.

"Oh, you're so gallant, officer," Nicholson offered with a very un-teacherly giggle.

Charlotte's wavering gaze fell on Pegg as he sat up from his shadowy corner.

He was rubbing his eyes and growling as if they burned him. Even in the lamplight Charlotte could see his face turning red with rising fury as he opened his mouth in a shout.

"Everyone here is under arrest!"

Charlotte froze for an instant, thinking for one wild moment that the spell hadn't worked and she had been found out. But as she looked, trembling, into Pegg's wide eyes, she realized that he was merely raving.

"Do you hear me? Listen to me, blast you! Surrender this instant."

His gaze was unfocused, and he seemed to look right through Charlotte. Brackenberry and Nicholson seemed as unaware of her presence as the unconscious vicar. They were all locked in the grip of the spell and, for the moment, Charlotte was safe.

"Ey?" Sophie suddenly snorted and cracked an eye open. She seemed to have fallen asleep again in Pegg's frozen arms but the door opening had roused her again. "What all this? What's going on then?" Her gaze fell on Brackenberry and she licked her lips. "Ah! Nice of you to pack lunch."

She stood up, rolled up her sleeves, and marched across the seat to seize Brackenberry's sleeve. To Charlotte's consternation, the brownie sank her jaws into the man's arm.

Charlotte's own gasp was lost under Brackenberry's explosion.

"What the blazes—?"

Miss Nicholson clutched his hand. "Are you all right, darling?"

Brackenberry looked puzzled for a moment, but he seemed oblivious to the small brownie dangling from his arm. "Tis nothing, my love, the mere pinch of an old war wound." He did give his arm a little shake, casting Sophie to the ground with a small thump.

Undeterred, the brownie stalked over to Brackenberry's boot and began gnawing on it.

"You might have brought sandwiches that were less stale," the brownie remarked to no one in particular as she rubbed her jaw after an unsuccessful chomp.

Charlotte gave herself a shake. She couldn't just stand there gawking, even if it was her first time to ever witness just what spell dust could do to a person. She had to relieve the Major of his papers while she still had the opportunity.

She reached cautiously across the carriage, her eyes never leaving the Major's confused face as she touched his satchel.

His stream of insults about some imaginary prisoner continued without pause. Charlotte took a steadying breath and flipped the satchel open.

"What's going on?" said an unfamiliar voice and Charlotte leaped back with a startled cry.

The body of the vicar shifted, and a figure struggled out from under him. The guard clambered to his knees and looked at Charlotte.

"You're letting in a draft, miss."

Charlotte stood frozen, with her hand gripping the door. Unlike the others, the guard was looking at her as if he knew her, and yet she didn't recognize him at all.

His face was altered. His formerly-dull eyes were feverishly bright and he *smiled* at her. No, he didn't smile—he grinned, beaming from ear to ear with a display of startlingly white teeth.

"That was a spell bomb, wasn't it? I thought it was, I've read about those but I've never seen one. Well chucked. Why *did* you chuck it, anyway?"

Charlotte opened and closed her mouth for a moment, wondering in a panic whether she ought to answer or not, and then her eye caught on the mumbling Pegg and the glint of metal as he drew his gun.

"Look out!" she gasped.

The guard twisted the gun out of the Major's hands with a swift motion and a cool expression.

"Never fear, young lady. No one will be shot while I'm here." He smiled at her again and proclaimed grandly. "I am Jack O' Lantern."

Still clutching at her heart and trying to recover from the image of a deranged Pegg shooting every last one of them, Charlotte looked at the guard in despair. Of all the fantasies he had to have, it *would* be that!

The guard slid closer to her, the lofty expression somewhat at odds with his smelly and bushy appearance.

"You can tell me what you were doing. And I think you'd better." He threw off his hat with a dramatic gesture usually reserved for tragedians in bad plays. "After all, Jack O Lantern is here!"

"Oh *no*," Charlotte groaned. She glanced around the bespelled carriage, feeling utterly outnumbered. But the one bright side was that no one would notice or care if she loaded Bates into the carriage.

She jumped from the carriage step onto the road again.

"Stop," the robot roused himself again. "You are not authorized to leave the carriage for any reason."

"Oh, would you *stop* it?" Charlotte grumbled. At least Bates was still lying on the ground outside the door where she had left him. Charlotte grabbed a limp arm and began the laborious process of heaving Bates into the carriage.

"New passenger?" the guard asked, sticking his head outside. "I hadn't realized we reached the station."

"Just help me, would you?" Charlotte grunted.

At least the spell dust had made the guard more cheerful. He grabbed an arm and did most of the loading himself.

"Brackenberry?" Pegg growled from his corner. "Have you arrested anyone yet?"

"I know we've only just met but may I call you Cordelia?" Brackenberry was asking Miss Nicholson as he stroked her hand.

"Of course you can, Edmund!" Nicholson tittered.

Sophie still seemed to believe that Brackenberry was some sort of snack and was doing her best to eat him with a spoon that she had produced from her pockets. When he proved to be unspoonable, she started striking him repeatedly with the implement in a fit of frustration.

Charlotte sat down in the carriage for a moment to catch her breath, and tried to think. There was only one clear route ahead of her. They had to drive on, and then perhaps she could rouse Bates at the crossroads and the two of them could escape while the robot drove the others to the nearest way station.

A poke roused her from her thoughts and she looked into the guard's grizzled face. "Hey,

I'm talking to you! What exactly are you up to, young woman?"

Charlotte looked into his eyes and resisted the urge to start laughing hysterically. "I have no idea."

The guard cocked his head. "Did you hear that?"

Charlotte managed to swallow back her nervous giggles and listened too.

Beyond the ravings and murmurings of their carriage mates, there was another voice.

Somewhere out there, on the moor, there was a rushing sound in the dark, like the roar of waves. Something huge and heavy and fast moving through the grass.

Charlotte glanced anxiously at the guard. He didn't look as cheerful anymore.

"What was that?" she quavered.

"You're not going to like the answer," the guard said grimly.

Then the noise struck the side of the carriage.

Charlotte found herself flung against the side of carriage, her face pressed close against the small window, her terrified eyes sweeping over her narrow view of the outside.

The lanterns on the top of the carriage were swinging wildly, and the shivering light glanced off a shadow that gleamed silver and scaly in the sudden illumination.

She might as well have been hit by the spell bomb, for Charlotte had lost all control of her limbs as a scream of horror rose in her throat, then stuck there in a helpless gargle.

The guard reached across her and slammed the window shutter shut.

"Will that keep it out?" Charlotte quavered.

"Not in the slightest," the guard told her.

The carriage shuddered, the wood structure cracking as something coiled itself around the wheels.

Charlotte whimpered. Why didn't the robot simply drive as fast as he possibly could? What was he doing up there?

Charlotte shoved the trap open and shouted at the robot. "Driver, what are you waiting for? Go!"

She peered up anxiously, trying to catch sight of the mechanical lump that should have been urging their vehicle on to safety. But she could see nothing above her but darkness.

Desperate, she crawled past the still-raving passengers to open the window shutter again, then recoiled, shrieking, against the guard.

As she opened the shutter, she had seen a mechanical head fly through the darkness, its tin top hat tumbling in the opposite direction. The coachmen had been battered to pieces.

"Oh, what *is* it?" Charlotte gasped. She grabbed the guard, "What *is* it?"

"Moor worms," the guard said grimly. "The spell bomb must have attracted them. Moor worms eat spell dust, didn't you know that?"

"No," Charlotte said, and then she was suddenly sobbing as the carriage shook again. "I don't know anything and I wish I were in bed and not sitting in a carriage with six lunatics and a coachman who thinks he's a hero. *When are we both going to realize that we're not heroes?*" Charlotte grabbed the coachman's arms and shook him. "When? *When?*"

The guard gave her a reproachful tap on the arm. "Now don't take on that way. You're getting hysterical."

"Yes," Charlotte sobbed. "I am."

This time it was the guard who shook Charlotte. "Pull yourself together!"

Charlotte gulped and glared at him reproachfully, but she stopped crying.

The carriage was struck again. Behind the sound of the impact, a hiss as loud and strong as wind wound its way through the windows as the occupants of the carriage went tumbling again.

"Are you all right, my love?" Brackenberry asked Miss Nicholson, obliviously elbowing Charlotte in his efforts to heave Miss Nicholson back into her seat.

"Oh, you're so gallant." Nicholson laid an arm on Brackenberry's arm. "I wonder why we fell. But yes, I'm fine."

"No, you're not fine!" Charlotte blurted out. "You're going to *die*."

"Hey, you get back here!' Sophie complained, crawling after Brackenberry and brandishing her spoon, interrupting the would-be-couples hug when she caused Brackenberry to howl in protest.

"Get off me, you fools!" Pegg snarled as he shoved aside the unconscious bodies of Bates and the vicar.

The guard's voice cut through the pandemonium like bright steel. "No one's going to die. Don't worry; it's nothing that the great Jack O' Lantern hasn't dealt with before."

Charlotte hit him in the arm as hard as she could. She had never hit anyone before. "Oh, would you stop saying that! You're not Jack O' Lantern!"

The guard shot her a superior look. "You audacious little snippet, of course I am!"

The thing outside struck the side of the carriage once more. Charlotte screamed as the carriage tilted sideways again, and for a moment she feared they would topple over entirely. She crawled over the others, trying to rebalance the vehicle by shifting to the other side.

"What are we going to *do*?" Charlotte whispered, then she realized who she was asking—six spell-bound passengers and a guard who thought he was Jack O' Lantern. She put her head in her hands and tried not to cry.

How had she wound up here? A few weeks ago, aside from the occasional worry, the greatest thing she had had to be afraid of was not embarrassing herself at social functions. And now here she was, throwing illegal spell bombs, trapped with strangers whose brains she had single-handedly turned to porridge, and stranded in the middle of the marsh with moor worms attacking her carriage.

The battering began again, more violently this time—one long horrible shaking in which Charlotte could do nothing but hold on with gritted teeth.

For a few moments, even the bespelled fools had to leave off their cursing and chewing and canoodling as they were flung willy-nilly across the interior of the coach.

Through the ordeal, the guard had an arm around Charlotte and kept speaking in a low, cheerful voice. "It's not so bad." The fourth time he said it, Charlotte said, "Would you please stop saying that!" But she clung to him all the same.

With a vicious jolt that nearly made Charlotte bit through her tongue, the carriage crashed down into the ruts of the road, upright once more.

Before Charlotte could even catch her breath, Jack elbowed her. "Enough of this knocking about. Tell me what you've been doing and what's going on."

In that moment, she didn't care that she was speaking to a mad guard. It was the first time anyone had asked her in days what was troubling her, and the trouble came spilling out in a shaky stream of words. "The major is going to have my brother arrested for writing pamphlets protesting against the government."

The guard's eyebrows flew up. "Your brother wrote those? He's the Voice of

Freedom?" He clapped her on the shoulders. "Good for him. Well, never fear, you'll both get out of this all right. If you can relieve the major of the incriminating papers, I'll handle the beasts. All right?"

"All . . . all right," Charlotte gulped. For the moment, it didn't matter whether this man was delusion or not—he *thought* he was on her side, and that meant he could be the ally she urgently needed. She only hoped he didn't get himself eaten.

"You had better take this." The guard pressed a pistol into Charlotte's hands. "Don't worry about me, I've got loads," he assured her, drawing his blunderbuss from over his shoulder and then kicking open the carriage door and somersaulting into the night with credible skill, considering his long coat.

Shaking, Charlotte shut the door after him and then turned her attention to Pegg, who was now lambasting the oblivious Brackenberry for dereliction of duty and threatening him with a flogging if he didn't start arresting people.

Charlotte strained to hear what was going on outside the carriage, but could hear nothing over the murmurings of Brackenberry and Nicholson, the barking of Pegg, and the grumbling of Sophie, who had now begun to sob angrily because her "food" was so tough.

"Everybody be quiet!" Charlotte shouted in frustration, but no one listened to her.

The rocking of the carriage had stopped, but it left an ominous silence in its wake.

Charlotte sat frozen between relief and consternation as she listened.

"Guard?" Charlotte hadn't thought to ask him his name. It occurred to her that the delusion person outside might not be answering to "guard" anymore and, feeling foolish, she called, "Jack? Jack O' Lantern?"

But there was only silence. That was good, wasn't it? As long as she didn't hear any screaming or biting that must mean the worms had left. It *had* to mean that.

And that meant Charlotte's task still needed doing, and could be done simply now that the carriage had stopped moving.

That was what she kept telling herself.

Shivering, Charlotte reached forward, one hand clutching the pistol while her free fingers fumbled with the latch of Pegg's satchel.

Pegg broke off in the middle of his tirade, and his head turned.

Charlotte froze as Pegg's hard grey eyes met hers.

"What are you doing?" He growled.

Charlotte raised her pistol, but Pegg was faster.

He seized her by the throat and began to squeeze.

Fear and pain shot through Charlotte with the same fierce explosion of the spell bomb as she clutched instinctively at the fingers wrapped around her throat.

"Help!" Charlotte gargled. "Someone help me!"

Brackenberry and Nicholson were still in one another's arms, murmuring sweet nothings. The brownie had now begun to chew on the immobile vicar's boots.

It was like something out of her nightmares. Charlotte had had dreams like this before, where her silent cries for help were ignored by the staring crowd looking on, oblivious to her plight.

Panic flooded her as her breath was snatching from her lungs. *This is it, I can't fight him. I'm going to die.*

And then, as if summoned, Richard's words flew through her clouded brain,

Sometimes, you have to hurt a bad man to save a good one.

"Give up, you little fool," Pegg hissed, shaking her gun hand, trying to force her to let go of the pistol.

"No!" Charlotte croaked. Remembering Bates, she pulled her foot back and drove it into Pegg's stomach as hard as she could.

Pegg doubled over, groaning and cursing her in a way that gave Charlotte the surge of anger she had so desperately needed.

Her fumbling hand found the pistol, and she seized it by the muzzle and brought the butt swinging around to strike Pegg in the temple.

His hands loosened, his nails scraping her throat as his fingers slipped free. Pegg toppled forward off his seat and onto the floor, stunned.

Gasping with relief, Charlotte clutched her throat, tears burning her eyes. She spared a quick glance for the still-oblivious passengers of the carriage with a sense of sudden resentment.

"You *idiots*," she grumbled. She knew it wasn't really their fault, but it still very much relieved her feelings.

Still shaking, Charlotte dipped her hand into the major's satchel, and this time nothing stopped her from removing the papers and cramming them into her pocket.

"I have it!" Charlotte called hoarsely to the still-silent driver. "Let's go, please!"

She flung the door open, without thinking, and then froze with her head half-out of the carriage, her heart hardening into a small, cold lump as she stared into the night.

Three marsh worms were in a semi-circle before the carriage door, silent and watching and hideous.

They looked like the dragons from old picture books, only smaller. They had no feet, but pushed through the sludge of the marsh like snakes. Their bodies were as big around as Charlotte's waist and their great horned heads, protruding jaws lined with razor-like teeth, and small red eyes that glowed like coals in their scaly faces, made Charlotte's stomach heave.

They watched her, swaying back and forth, with a low rumble issuing from their throats.

Charlotte pressed back, fear drubbing in her chest and throat. She wanted to close her eyes, but she was incapable of moving. She could barely breathe.

But, shooting through the terror like a lance through a boil, was the sudden realization that the people behind her were completely defenseless and the guard was out here on his own. It was up to her to save them. She had to do something.

She raised her pistol with trembling hands, then a calm cool voice struck her motionless.

"Don't shoot," said the guard.

Charlotte turned, and looked up.

Jack was standing on top of the driver's box, coat snapping in the wind, hat off, and gloves somehow gone. He was holding something in his hand, a kind of glowing rod, with long tails of shimmering light trailing from it, like ribbons of fire, and in its flare Charlotte could see him smiling.

With his bare hand, Jack seized one of the ribbons, and pulled it free of the rod with a crack that sounded like lightning. He threw the ribbon with a hard snap, and it sailed through the air like an arrow let loose from a string.

The three worms twisted in its direction and then their heads dropped down into the reeds with a rush of motion that made Charlotte's stomach drop into her feet.

With a rush of sound, the worms tunneled away, leaving the marsh reeds churning and writhing in their wake as they headed towards the distant glow of the magic ribbon. And just like that, they disappeared.

Charlotte gulped and leaned back against the carriage, shutting her eyes briefly and then opening them again, trembling with a sudden relief of nerves as she confirmed that the worms really were gone, and they were all still alive.

She turned to the guard, stammering. "That was . . .that was amazing. How did you do that? I was told that every mortal reacts to spell dust differently but—"

"Precisely." The guard looked down at her and smiled, an expression that completely transformed his face. "I'm not mortal."

His beard appeared to be half-torn from his face and he reached up a long thin hand to pull it away, revealing a clean-shaven face. His hat had fallen off during the debacle and, in the glimmer of the lantern, Charlotte could see the tips of his pointed ears.

Charlotte sucked in a choking breath.

"Jack O' Lantern?"

The guard who was not a guard winked at her. "I already told you that."

Charlotte clutched at the door to keep from falling over. "But . . . but you're in prison."

Jack shook his head. "The reports of my capture were greatly exaggerated. Or, at least, falsified. They have the wrong man in jail."

Charlotte stared at him. As utterly relieved as she was to discover that Jack O' Lantern was free and at large, it immediately occurred to Charlotte that the poor fellow currently locked in irons was bearing another man's punishment.

"The man they've caught," she blurted out, "the one they think is you—are you going to rescue him?"

Jack gave her a mildly reproving look. "Of course I am."

Charlotte ducked her head, embarrassed—but also nursing a little glow of hope and trust inside herself that she hadn't felt so implicitly since she was a child. Of *course* Jack O' Lantern would save the man. That's what Jack O' Lantern did.

Everything would be all right now.

"What do we do now?" Charlotte asked shyly.

Jack jumped down from the carriage to stand beside her. Charlotte nearly pinched herself. She was standing beside the real live Jack O' Lantern.

She blushed when she remembered how she had spoken to him in the carriage.

As if guessing her thoughts, Jack smiled, his face mischievous, but his words were kind. "You did well, miss. And don't worry about your brother. I'm going to save him. I was aware that Major Pegg had incriminating papers. That's why I'm here."

"Y-you *knew*? You were going to save him? It would have turned out all right even if I hadn't . . .?" Charlotte pressed a hand to her temples. "I should have never tried to help at all," she whispered. "I only made things more difficult for you."

"Nonsense! Bates owes his life to you, not to me. If it hadn't been for your quick thinking, he would have been shot. I was struggling with that idiot robot while you were luring the glow bugs to sleep. A lot can happen in a few moments but, fortunately, you were there."

Charlotte raised her head; the doubt brushed away by Jack's words as easily as she had brushed away the glow flies, and with the glow of pride came a rush of clarity. She looked at Jack with sudden suspicion. "Did you put all those Voice of Freedom pamphlets on our persons at the way station?"

"That was me," Jack confessed peacefully. "It was my calling card. I like my victims to have a little warning of what the caper of the night is going to be."

Charlotte grinned. "The look on the major's face when he felt his pocket was wonderful."

Jack laughed. "I thought it might be." He clapped his hands together. "Now, let's attend to the coachmen's remains, shall we?"

Once again, Charlotte was struck by a wave of unreality as she helped the Jack O' Lantern heave the robot onto the road and disassemble its remaining parts so that Jack could haul it to some service station and have the poor thing repaired.

Jack put a hand on her shoulder, praising her quick work as she unscrewed an arm and Charlotte nearly had to pinch herself.

A few days ago, she had been a shy squire's daughter, doing as she was bidden and working at her music and stitchery. Tomorrow she would still be a good daughter, and would still be working at her music and her stitchery. But she now knew just what she was made off. She wasn't a coward. Richard would be so proud of her. And, for the first time that she could remember in a long while, Charlotte was proud of herself.

Jack finished bundling the robot parts into a haversack and straightened up. "That's that. Now we just have to get you and the unfortunate lunatics inside this rig safely to town. I'd drive you there, but I'm reluctant to take Bates into the village."

"You're needed elsewhere, anyway," Charlotte protested automatically. "*I* can drive the carriage into town." She had never driven one before, let alone across the Moor, but she felt a sudden reckless confidence. After facing down an officer of the law, glow flies, moor worms, and spell-crazed passengers, she felt she could handle a mechanical rig.

"And your story when you arrive without your driver?" Jack asked, his eyebrows raised slightly as he looked her up and down, taking her measure.

Charlotte straightened to her full height, determined to show that he could trust her. "Why, I'll just pretend that I was hit with the spell bomb and got it into my head that I was a coachman and knocked the robot off his seat and left him on the road in a fit of madness."

Jack nodded approvingly. "That's using your head, Miss Morrison. Here, this might add credence to your claim at temporary insanity." He picked up the robot's top hat and popped it on top of Charlotte's head. It nearly fell off again as Charlotte burst out laughing. She felt ridiculous, but it was rather exciting to feel ridiculous.

She helped Jack O' Lantern haul poor Bates out of the carriage. The elf lifted the man easily over one shoulder, preparing to carry him into the night, and to safety.

"One last thing," said Jack. "Those papers. I'll take care of them."

Charlotte handed over the papers that incriminated her brother without hesitation. Jack met her gaze with a look that told her she could have faith that all would be well.

"I know a lot of creatures that enjoy snacking on paper." He tucked them into his coat. "These won't see the light of day. I swear."

Charlotte believed him. "Aren't you coming along for a little while?" she asked without thinking, "to keep to the road?"

Jack smiled and shook his head. "I make my own roads." His eyes turned out towards the dark for a moment. "This is my marsh."

Of course it was—he was the last elf, the great Jack O' Lantern. Charlotte knew that, but she was simply reluctant to see him go. Once he walked off into the night, this night of discovery would all be over, and she would never see the hero again.

At least she could be grateful that she had seen him at all.

Charlotte managed a smile and said with all her heart, "Good luck, Jack O' Lantern."

Jack turned swiftly back towards her; his smile brilliant. "Why thank you, Miss Charlotte. I appreciate it."

Charlotte hiked up her skirts and clambered up onto the driver's box, looking down at the driver's panel, familiarizing herself with the steering.

"You've done well tonight, miss," said Jack, looking up at her. "You acted fast, even when you didn't know how things would turn out. And you were willing to sacrifice yourself for someone else—even over the needs of your own brother." Jack tilted his head. "That's a rare kind of selflessness, Miss Morrison."

Charlotte suddenly felt a little like a glow fly—shining and as light as air.

Jack looked at her with twinkling eyes. "You know . . . I always need new recruits, official ones, that is . . . If you're interested."

Charlotte's heart leaped. She had thought the adventure was over.

But now she saw that it had only just begun.

"I'll be in touch." Jack dipped his head to her, carefree and dashing and more than ready to strike out into the night to smuggle one man to safety and then free another from prison before the night was out. Charlotte had one last glimpse of his wild, merry face, his eyes and teeth brilliant in the moonlight with an otherworldly glow, living up to his name of

Jack O' Lantern in every way. "You sure you can manage, Miss Morrison?"

Charlotte turned the switch that turned on the engine and, to her delight, felt the carriage rattle beneath her, ready to run. She gripped the controls, and gave the pedals a little push, feeling the carriage respond to her.

"Why yes, Jack," she said, with a dawning surprise as the unfamiliar feeling of complete confidence swept over her. "I do believe I can!"

About the Author:

Allison Tebo is a writer committed to creating magical stories full of larger-than-life characters, a dash of grit, and plenty of laughs. She is one of the contributors of *A Villains Ever After,* and her contribution to the series—*The Goblin and the Dancer*—went on to become a Realm Makers Readers' Choice Finalist. She went on to spearhead the multi-author series, *A Classic Retold*, and her epic fantasy retelling of Beowulf, *Break the Beast,* which went on to win the ChristLit Award. She has also written the *Tales of Ambia,* a series of comedic fairy tale retellings and co-runs the speculative fiction e-zine *Worlds of Adventure.* Allison graduated with merit from London Art College and, when not creating new worlds with words or paint, she enjoys reading, baking, and making lists. To find out more, you can visit her at her website www.allisonteboauthor or find her on Instagram @allisonteboauthor

www.ingramcontent.com/pod-product-compliance
Lightning Source LLC
LaVergne TN
LVHW012037060526
838201LV00061B/4659